RICHARD SCARRY'S
Best Two-Minute Stories Ever!

The Best Bedtime Stories Featuring Favorite Animal Friends

A GOLDEN BOOK • NEW YORK
Western Publishing Company, Inc., Racine, Wisconsin 53404

 Library of Congress Catalog Card Number: 89-80144 ISBN: 0-307-12186-0 ISBN: 0-307-62186-3 (lib. bdg.)
B C D E F G H I J K L M

CHIPMUNK'S BIRTHDAY PARTY

It was Chipmunk's birthday. He invited his friends to come to his birthday party. When they came, he said, "Hi, Rabbit! Hi, Mouse! Hi, Goat! Hi, Donkey! Hi, Frog!"

"Now, just a minute," said Mommy Chipmunk. "There'll be no birthday party until your ears are clean!"

Bunny Rabbit has big ears to clean, hasn't he?

Chipmunk and Mouse helped Mommy in the kitchen. Mommies always have to work hard when they give birthday parties.

All the children went outside to play. Chipmunk went sailing on the pond with Rabbit. They wore life jackets. They wanted to be safe just in case they should fall overboard.

Then they all played leapfrog.

It was time to stop playing games. It was time to eat ice cream and drink lemonade. They all put on funny hats.

Mouse picked some flowers. He gave them to Mommy Chipmunk to thank her for the birthday party. What a nice Mouse! Do you have nice birthday parties, too?

THE FISHING CAT

A cat went down to the sea to fish. He wanted to catch a whale.

Did he catch a big, big whale?

No! He caught a big, big log.

Did he toss the log back into the sea? No. The cat did not. He took out his knife and he cut the log. He cut it here and there. Now, why did the cat do that?

He did it to make a fine fishing boat.

So LOOK OUT all you whales!

THE HOUSE OF MISTRESS MOUSE

This is the house of Mister Mouse. He lived all alone and he was very lonely. One day he received a letter from Mistress Mouse. The letter said:

"Dear Mister Mouse, I am lonely, too. Will you please come and visit me? Love and kisses, Mistress Mouse."

Mister Mouse said to himself, "I would like very much to visit Mistress Mouse, but I don't know where she lives. However, I will just have to get into my little car and go look for her.

"There is a house just ahead," said Mister Mouse. "Perhaps that is where Mistress Mouse lives."

He knocked on the door. "Is this the house of Mistress Mouse?" he asked. Mister Mouse was very frightened, for that was the house of...

"MEOWWWRRR!"

...the house of Mister Cat!

"What a cute little mouse," thought Mister Cat as he watched him speed away in his car. "I wonder why he was so frightened." But Mister Mouse knew better than to go into Mister Cat's house. Didn't he?

Soon he came to a bright red barn. He knocked on the barn door. It was the house of...

"CUT-CUT-CUT-CU-DAHCUT!"

...it was the house of Mrs. Hen and her baby chicks. "Please don't bother me. I am teaching my chicks to scratch," she said.

And so the mouse traveled on.

Finally he came to a cute little house on a lovely country lane. He knocked on the pretty little yellow door. "Is this the house of Mistress Mouse?" he asked. The door slowly opened.

Sure enough! It WAS the house of Mistress Mouse!

And they were soon married by Preacher Mole. Mister Mouse gave Mistress Mouse a golden wedding ring with a bright diamond on top. And from that day on they were never lonely. They went on picnics. They took rides in the country. They went rowing on the lake.

And then one night, after they had finished their supper, they heard something. It was a tiny "squeak, squeak, squeak," coming from the bedroom. What do you suppose it was that was squeaking?

It was their BABY!

He wanted to be kissed good night!

"Good night, Daddy Mouse."

"Good night, Mommy Mouse."

"Good night, Baby Mouse."

"Good night."

THE EGG IN THE HOLE

One day, up in the hayloft of the barn, Henny laid an egg. The egg rolled through a hole in the floor to a room below.

"Oh, my! I hope I haven't lost it!" she said.

Henny rushed down the stairs to the room below.

"Have you seen my egg?" asked Henny.

"Yes, I have," said Billy Goat. "It fell on my ice cream. Then it rolled along the table and went out the window."

Henny hurried to the window.

“Have you seen my egg?” she asked.

“Yes, I have,” said Little Bird. “It rolled along the rain gutter and then went down the hole.”

Henny ran outside to where Pig was sitting.

“Have you seen my egg?” asked Henny. “I’m afraid I have lost it.”

“Your egg just hit me on the head,” said Pig. “It rolled down my back, through my curly tail, and across the barnyard.”

Henny rushed across the barnyard. She saw her egg just before it rolled into a hole in the ground.

Just then from out of the hole appeared a tiny mouse.

"Henny," he said, "I have found your egg! Something special happened....It is broken, and it is in a lot of pieces!

"BUT...if you look closely...you will see that you have a brand-new baby chick in its place!" Henny was so pleased! She had lost her egg, but now she had a baby chick instead.

You would be pleased, too, wouldn't you?

"Hi, Mommy," said Baby Chick.

I AM A BUNNY

I am a bunny. My name is Nicholas. I live in a hollow tree.

In the spring, I like to pick flowers.

In the summer, I listen to the insects buzzing and humming.

In the fall, I like to watch the leaves falling from the trees.

And, when winter comes, I watch the snow falling from the sky.

Then I curl up in my hollow tree and dream about spring.

THE FOX AND THE CROW

A crow sat high in a tree, holding a tasty bit of cheese in her mouth. Along came a warthog.

"The crow will laugh when she sees my funny face," he said. "And then when she laughs, she'll drop the cheese."

He called to the crow, making a funny face.

But she didn't even smile.

Along came a hungry little elephant. "Drop the cheese to me, Crow," said the elephant, "or I will give you a shower bath."

But the crow did not drop the cheese, even though—*WHOOSH!*—the elephant's trunk sent up a stream of water.

Along came a hungry big brown bear.

"Drop the cheese to me," called the big brown bear, "and you may have this pot of honey." But the crow did not like honey, and she did not drop the cheese.

The crow was about to eat the cheese when along came a cunning little fox.

"Oh, beautiful Crow," he called, "you are lovely to see. A bird with such charming feathers must sing a pretty tune. Please sing for me."

Now, the crow had never been told she was beautiful, although she thought she was. And she had never been told that her voice was pretty. She opened her beak and rasped an ugly *"CAAW!"*

Down tumbled the cheese, into the fox's mouth! Now, wasn't she a silly bird to let that sweet talk fool her?

THE BUNNY STORY

Daddy Bunny tossed his baby in the air. "What will our baby be when he grows up?" asked Daddy Bunny.

Baby Bunny just smiled at his bunny family. He knew what he would be.

Great Uncle Bunny wanted the baby to be an engineer on a big train. "He would ring the bell when he was ready to start the train, and blow his horn—Toot! Toot!—in the tunnels," said Great Uncle Bunny.

But the baby bunny did not want to be an engineer on a big train when he grew up. He nibbled on his carrot and looked wise. He knew what he wanted to be.

"I think our bunny should be an airplane pilot," said the little bunny's sister. "What fun to jump out of his plane in a parachute!"

"Maybe he will be a fire fighter," said Great Aunt Bunny. "He could drive a big truck to all the fires."

"He may grow up to be a farmer with a fine red tractor," said Uncle Bunny.

But the baby bunny did not want to be an airplane pilot or a fire fighter or a farmer with a fine red tractor when he grew up. He bounced on his daddy's knee and laughed. Can you guess what he will be?

He will have lots of little bunny children to feed when they are hungry. He will read them a story when they are sleepy, and tuck them into bed at night.

And that is what the baby bunny will grow up to be: a daddy rabbit.

Two One-Minute Stories That Make Up Two Minutes!

A DOG AND HIS BONE

A little dog hurried to the stream with a large juicy bone in his mouth. He wanted to eat the bone all by himself. So he ran across the log that bridged the stream. Then, in the water, he saw a picture of himself. But he thought it was another dog.

"Ah, now I shall have two nice bones to eat," thought the greedy little dog. He growled and snapped at the other bone. SPLASH! His bone fell into the water. And so did he! Now he had nothing to eat. Greedy-greedy makes a hungry puppy.

THERE WAS AN OLD WOMAN

There was an old woman
tossed up in a basket,
Seventeen times as high as
the moon.
Where she was going I
couldn't but ask it,
For under her arm she carried
a broom.
Old woman, old woman, old
woman, said I,
Where are you going to up
so high?
To sweep the cobwebs out of
the sky,
And I'll be with you by and by.

GOOD NIGHT, LITTLE BEAR

It is time for Little Bear to go to bed. Mother Bear closes the storybook. She gives Little Bear a good-night kiss.

Then over to his big furry father runs the little bear. Wheee! Father Bear swings his little one high up to his shoulders for a ride to bed.

"Duck your head," calls Mother Bear just in time. And into the snug little bedroom they go.

Squeak! The tiny bed sighs as Father Bear sits down. "Now, into bed with you," he says. He waits for Little Bear to climb down. But Little Bear doesn't move. He sits up on his father's shoulders and grins. Father Bear waits. He yawns a rumbly yawn. Is Father Bear falling asleep? No. Suddenly he opens his eyes again.

"Why, I must have been dreaming," says Father Bear, pretending to wake up. But what's this? Father Bear looks under the pillow. Nobody there. He doesn't seem to feel something tickling his ear.

Aha. There's a lump down under the blanket. Father Bear pats the lump. But it doesn't squeak or wiggle. Can it be Little Bear? Why, it's the toy teddy and the blue bunny waiting for Little Bear to come to bed!

"Mother, that naughty bear is hiding," says Father Bear to Mother Bear with a wink. "Now, where is that naughty bear hiding? He wouldn't run away. Not a little bear hungry for chocolate cake!"

And that big daddy bear cuts himself a huge piece of chocolate cake right under the little bear's nose! Little Bear suddenly feels hungry. But, just then, Father Bear stops smack in front of the mirror.

"Why, there he is!" roars the big bear.

"But you couldn't find me," squeaks Little Bear, reaching for the chocolate cake.

"But I've found you now," says Father Bear. Little Bear wiggles and giggles under his daddy's strong arm...all the way into bed.

"Did I really fool you, Daddy?" asks Little Bear. Father Bear just laughs and winks. Do you think Father Bear knew all the time?